Theodore J. Eckerson

When my Ship Comes in

and other rhymes of camp and hearth

.

Theodore J. Eckerson

When my Ship Comes in
and other rhymes of camp and hearth

ISBN/EAN: 9783337394936

Printed in Europe, USA, Canada, Australia, Japan

Cover: Foto ©Andreas Hilbeck / pixelio.de

More available books at **www.hansebooks.com**

WHEN MY SHIP COMES IN,

AND OTHER RHYMES OF CAMP AND HEARTH.

BY

MAJOR THEO. J. ECKERSON,

UNITED STATES ARMY.

CAMBRIDGE:

Printed at the Riverside Press.

1881.

PREFACE AND DEDICATION.

THESE rhymes are now, at the request of friends whose judgment is perhaps warped by their partiality, thrown together in their present form. Criticism upon these effusions is not invited, as no poetic merit whatever is claimed for them. They are simply *rhymes*, jotted down from time to time, and extending over many years.

Such as they are I dedicate them to

MY BELOVED WIFE,

my constant and faithful companion in my journeys North, South, East, and West, — on the ocean, over mountain snows, and across rivers and plains, — in the performance of my public duties during the past thirty-three years.

THEODORE J. ECKERSON.

NORFOLK HOUSE,
BOSTON HIGHLANDS,
July, 1881.

CONTENTS.

——◆——

WHEN MY SHIP COMES IN.

I 'VE a precious little daughter,
   And her name is Adelaide, —
No bright jewels yet I 've bought her,
   Though her nut-brown hair 's in braid;
And as often as she plagues me
   For a bracelet or a pin,
I console her with the promise,
   " *Yes, love, when my ship comes in !* "

Oh, the dreaming little daughter!
   In bright visions of the night,
Strings of fairest pearls and bracelets
   Still appear before her sight,
And before the morning kisses
   Or the morning prayers begin,
Up she runs to ask her father
   When the ship is coming in.

" Listen, mother, let me tell you
    What a pleasant dream I 've had :
Up the straits came father's vessel,
    And you both appeared *so* glad ;
All the bells in town were ringing,
    And away above the din
I could read on floating banners,
    ' *Joy ! The ship is coming in !*'

" Then methought a host of bright ones,
    As the anchor rattled down,
Gathered in the shrouds, and, cheering,
    Joined the huzzas of the town ;
While the Captain, smiling sweetly,
    By a gesture of his hand
Had the sails all furled so neatly
    By a white-winged angel band ! "

Dream on, joyous little daughter,
    But a few, short, sunny years,
And your visions bright will vanish,
    . All your pearls dissolve in tears ;
For the long-expected vessel
    Bears no pearl nor jeweled pin,
Though her freight of tears and sadness
    Is most surely coming in.

Yes, my trusting little daughter,
  Oh, my winsome Adelaide,
When I cross the troubled water,
  And my last, last debt is paid,
When sad faces crowd around me,
  And, with locks all white and thin,
I am laid within my coffin,
  Then my ship is coming in!

Of her freight of tears and sorrows
  None will be for me to share;
Mine have all been wept and suffered
  Through long years of grief and care;
Yours will be the cross, my darling,
  While the crown alone I win;
Yours will be the tears and anguish,
  When my ship comes sailing in!

For my great Redeemer liveth!
  He who stilled the raging seas
Steers the ship that fills your dreamings,
  And controls each adverse breeze;
He who bore the cross, my Addie,
  To redeem a world from sin,
Always smiles to find us ready
  When the ship is coming in.

To my ear, this pleasant evening,
  Sitting here before the door,
Heavy anchor-chains are rattling,
  As my ship comes near the shore;
I can hear the loose sails flapping,
  And the sailors' merry din,
And I see the Captain smiling
  As my ship sails slowly in !

June, 1861.

COMING OVER THE BAR

AT THE MOUTH OF THE COLUMBIA RIVER.

I PROMISED to tell you, my little star,
  Some night before you slept,
Of the morn we sailed in over the bar,
  And the reason why I wept
That day, when others all seemed so glad,
And I in the state-room sat, so sad.

Was it that friends would meet me there,
  Friends who had known me long?
That cordial smiles, with a greeting rare,
  Would come from that merry throng?
All these, my sweet one, I knew were here —
But not for them was the falling tear.

Away on Astoria's rugged height,
  As the steamship dashed through the wave,
I could see the mound, with its head-board white,
  That covers your brother's grave;

I could fancy I heard, as the ship came nigh,
The angel voice of our first-born boy!

The wild sea-gull floated swiftly past,
  And uttered its plaintive cry;
The great bar foamed in the fiendish blast,
  And reared its white mountains high;
But above them all, on the swelling gale,
I could hear my dead boy's mournful wail.

Swift back to the past I wandered then,
  To the scene of that stormy day
When I mournfully followed the precious one,
  And they lowered him into the clay,
While tears were blent with the prayers then said,
As I strewed the roses over his bed.

Ten long years have gone slowly by,
  Well checkered with grief and joy;
Such tears have seldom bedimmed my eye
  As flowed for that gentle boy,
When I gazed once more on that lonely grave,
On the fir-crown'd height by the sounding wave.

Five other precious ones now have twined
  Their tendrils about my heart:

God ! In Thy mercy still be kind,
   For oh, 't is *so* hard to part !
Leave me my loving ones treading the sod ;
Keep Thou the little one gone back to God !

Yes, my own sweet one, my friends were there, —
   Friends who had known me long ;
The cordial smile and the greeting rare
   Came from that merry throng ;
But you now know why, when all seemed glad,
I sat in the state-room, lone and sad.

   February 5, 1862.

NINETEEN YEARS.

Nineteen years, dear Lizzie, on their course
    have run
Since our vows were plighted, — vows that made
    us one ;
Oh the clouds, the sunshine — Oh the smiles, the
    tears —
Oh the joys, the sorrows, of those nineteen years !

Heaven hath kindly lent us, as our path we 've
    trod,
Little hearts to love us, little souls from God ;
Some still travel with us up the mountain steep :
These are left to love us — *one* is laid to sleep !

He, our precious first-born, pearl of all the rest,
Waits within the portals of the ever blest,
Watching for the coming of the loved of earth,
Those who rocked his cradle ere his second
    birth !

Oh, that night of horror when his spirit fled,
And we sat despairing, watching with our dead,
Vainly, madly clinging to our darling one —
Holding back the answer, *"God! Thy will be
     done!"*

.   .   .   .

Nineteen years have taught us that with bleed-
     ing feet
Thorny paths are trodden, though the flowers be
     sweet!
Cups of woe are given — hours of deep distress,
Pointing us to heaven, home of happiness.

.   .   .   .

Nineteen years, dear Lizzie, thus their course
     have sped, —
Do I love thee better than when first we wed?
Couldst thou read this heart, love, thou wouldst
     joy to see
Not a warm pulsation there but throbs for thee!

When fatigued and sickened with life's many
     snares,
Ah, full well. thou knowest how to soothe my
     cares!
On that faithful bosom I recline my head,
All the world forgetting — all my troubles fled!

Thou, who liv'st for others — thou, who, oft in
　　pain,
Still art self-forgetting, others' health to gain ;
Thou, whose intuition, when I 'm prone to stray,
Sees the hidden danger — points the better way ;

Thou, my guardian spirit in all times of need,
Could I cease to love thee I were lost indeed !
Could thy gentle nature for one moment doubt,
Hope would flee, and sunshine from our lives
　　fade out !

Nineteen years, dear Lizzie !　Oh, through many
　　more
May we walk together to that better shore,
Where the thornless roses of a world of bliss
Shall make up in sweetness for the thorns of
　　this !

November, 1867.

EPITHALAMIUM.

No clouds hang o'er thy future, — thy sky is
    clear and bright,
Yet silent tears are falling, loved one, for thee
    to-night!
A father's heart is swelling, grief mingles with
    his mirth, —
Grief, that so soon thou leavest the old familiar
    hearth!

A mother gazes on thee with all a parent's pride,
And pleasure fills her bosom — she sees her
    girl a bride!
But ah! a shade of sadness comes stealing o'er
    her brow,
She mournfully remembers one place is *vacant
now!*

Thou, in her weary moments hast been a com-
    forter;
Thy day-dreams and child-sorrows were all re-
    vealed to her;

2

Thou wert the first fair daughter that in her
    arms she pressed,
And oh! 't is sad to give thee in other arms to
    rest.

Fond sisters, too, and brothers are watching thee
    with joy;
No antepast of sadness their pleasure can alloy;
They see that thou art happy — no tear bedims
    thine eye —
Thou 'rt with them now, but sadly they 'll miss
    thee by and by!

Thy chosen lord is gazing with rapture on that
    form
That turns to meet his glances in rapture just as
    warm!
His heart was formed for loving a soul like
    thine, sweet dove!
But were his bosom marble, to see thee were to
    love!

Go with him, then, fair flower! cling with thy
    youthful soul
To him who swears to guard thee to life's un-
    certain goal;

May happiness attend thee while gliding down
    the stream,
And all thy days be pleasant as a pure infant's
    dream !

HOME JOYS AND SORROWS.

COME, prattling little one,
  Come to thy father's arms,
For day's dull toil is done,
  And home is full of charms.

Leap, my young soldier, leap!
  Shout forth thy joy with might!
How sweet will be the sleep
  That crowns thy lids to-night!

Thy brother looked like thee,
  Ere God his spirit took;
Not quite so full of glee,
  But ah, that heavenly look!

Yes, and we loved him, too
  (Frown not, we loved another),
And God, who took him, knew
  How we did love thy brother;

And how we watched him grow,
  Through months that slowly ran,
And longed together, so,
  To see our boy a man ;

And when the fell disease
  Was preying on his cheek,
How, on our bended knees,
  Our souls' distress we'd speak :

" Live, little darling, live,
  Thy father's fondest trust,
For, oh, we cannot give
  Thy beauty to the dust !

" Father in heaven ! look down,
  In mercy hear our prayer,
We may deserve thy frown,
  But, ah, in pity spare ! "

In vain our fond regard,
  Affliction's vale we trod ;
And, though the task was hard,
  We gave him back to God.

Thy mother's hopeless grief
  Long time no comfort knew,

Till Heaven a sweet relief
Upon our misery threw.

And *thou* wert sent to cheer
Our sad, benighted way,
And with thy smile to clear
Our darkness into day.

Oh, words of joy were there !
And tears, like sunshine rain,
To chase away despair —
We clasped our boy again !

The little toys, long hidden
Within the secret drawer,
Came out, almost unbidden,
Once more to strew the floor.

.   .   .   .   .   .

Ah ! sleepy little one,
Thine eyelids droop, I see ;
Well, father's story 's done,
And mother waits for thee.

God love thy precious heart,
And keep thee with us long ;

But if we 're called to part,
　God! make the weak heart strong!

See how the dear one smiles,
　As if our prayer to Heaven
Had reached the blessed aisles,
　And answer sweet were given.

There, fold thy little hands
　And sleep ; come, take him, mother;
He 'll dream of heavenly lands,
　And see his angel brother !

July, 1852.

THE GOOD MAN.

WHO is the good man? Is it he
　　Who, conscious of superior power,
Ignores himself, that he may be
　　Of use to others every hour?

Certes, the man who thus would use
　　His powers to aid his fellow-man,
Who ne'er his influence would refuse
　　The flame of human love to fan,

Must bear a larger, loftier soul
　　Than millions of our selfish race,
Who only seek to reach their goal
　　By means however low and base.

Then let us contemplate this man,
　　Though his existence be ideal ;
And, while with earnest thought we scan
　　His points, imagine he is real.

Would he be tender? Or be stern?
　Patient? Or full of fretfulness?
Quick for his vested rights to turn,
　And fierce those vested rights to press?

Would he neglect the claims of others,
　To nurse with jealousy his own?
Or, judging all mankind as brothers,
　Stand up, sometimes, for theirs alone?

Extreme to mark what's done amiss
　Against himself? Or patient when
His wrongs are greatest? Seeking bliss
　In righting wrongs of other men?

Fickle in temper? Losing head
　For every fool that wags the tongue?
Thrown off his balance by the dread
　Of wit's frail shaft against him flung?

I tell thee, friend, that not one fool,
　Nor all the fools arrayed together,
Could turn that man of brow so cool;
　My friend, the good man is no feather?

His well-poised temper never fails;
　He cannot lose his self-respect;

And when the storm of wrath assails,
    He stands, in conscious strength, erect.

He bears with peevish ones, and makes
    Allowance for the soul that's weak;
Ingratitude he calmly takes,
    And smiles at insolence's freak.

He shuns the dark, revengeful mood,
    And by fresh kindness nobly given,
O'ercomes the evil by his good, —
    All-powerful attribute of Heaven!

In short, no fiendish hate without,
    And no ill-temper throned within,
Can turn this noble one about,
    Nor from his path this brave one win.

For inborn generosity
    Can tread no pathway save its own;
Benevolence, pure-souled and free,
    Smiles at the dirt before it thrown!

Yes, let us dream of such a man,
    A tower of magnanimity,
Whose lofty soul with ease may scan
    What others can but dimly see!

Haply our dreams, by Morphean arts
Unknown to shallow mortal ken,
May graft his virtues on our hearts,
And make us better, happier men.

TO SALLIE.

Go, precious daughter, though our hearts are griev-
    ing !
  Go with the warrior husband of thy choice,
Nor heed the pangs that pierce us at thy leaving,
  As now we say " Farewell ! " with faltering voice.

God's blessing go with thee, our darling daughter,
  And shelter thee from evil on thy way !
Watch over thee upon the stormy water,
  And be thy guard, thy guide, thy life-long stay.

And oh, when absent from the hearts that love
    thee,
  And from the eyes that watched thee from thy
    birth,
Let memories of the absent ones oft move thee
  To holy thoughts amid the scenes of mirth.

Think of that mother who with pure devotion
  Has guided thy young steps from infancy ;

Whose breast is fraught with love as vast as ocean,
    And swells with grief at parting now from thee.

Think of thy father! how his loved ones wander
    And leave his waning years to loneliness ;
Yet, though the ties of love with age grow fonder,
    Submissively he parts with thy caress.

This sad farewell is not a hopeless parting ;
    Not his thy mother's pangs of rayless grief ;
To him the throbbing breast, the tear-drop starting,
    Are but the harbingers of kind relief.

For he has watched with joy his bright young
      vision,
    As onward sped her years to womanhood,
And knew that love must soon assert its mission,
    With all its scenes of evil and of good.

Think of thy absent sister, and thy brothers,
    Who prize thee with a love beyond compare ;
Thy only sister, who, above all others,
    Will sadly miss thy form at bedside prayer.

And now thou goest with thy brave young soldier,
    To meet the storms of earth-life by his side ;

One who has sworn within his arms to fold you,
  And shield e'en with his life his fair young
    bride.

Farewell, my daughter, and our prayers attend
    thee ;
  Heed not the tears that will unbidden flow.
May Heaven its fairest, dearest blessing send thee ;
  Go, with our tears, our prayers, our blessings, —
    go !

January 31, 1878.

FAREWELL ADDRESS.

WRITTEN FOR, AND RECITED BY, MRS. JULIA DEAN HAYNE,
ON THE OCCASION OF HER FAREWELL BENEFIT, AT PORT-
LAND, OREGON, NOVEMBER 12, 1864.

THE actress comes, not now to act a part,
But speak the feelings of a grateful heart
For kindly smiles, and your too warm applause,
So richly given, yet in so poor a cause.
She acts not now, but feelings, oh, how strong!
Rush to find utterance from her feeble tongue.

The unremitting toil, the anguish deep,
In midnight study oft, while others sleep,
Till, all fatigued, the overburdened brain
Finds respite short, and wakes to toil again, —
Wakes to the cares that claim from her their due,
As wife, as mother, and as actress too.
The dread which visits oft the fainting heart,
Lest all her efforts fail to fill the part ;
Lest, while the stern endeavors of the mind
Are sadly tasked, the portrait true to find,

And paint with truth each passion's varying hue,
The faults might glare, her pictures prove un-
　　　true ;
These wring the heart, and none save artists know
Those bitter, bitter depths of mental woe.
But, oh, what sweet results have met her here,
To banish all anxiety and fear !
All care to-night is scattered to the wind, .
Your smiles to greet, your kind applause to find.
Thanks for the welcome thus extended here,
From eyes that sparkle with true friendly cheer.
Here, where the bright Willamette wanders free,
To seek its goal far in the Northern sea,
And, like some fair and blushing mountain bride,
Greet with the nuptial kiss old Ocean's tide ;
Here, where the hardy miner rests awhile,
Returning from the scenes of honest toil,
To wait the noble vessel, soon to bear
His earth-dug treasures for loved ones to share ;
Here, as I mark your city's busy scene,
With joy I hail Pacific's second queen !

Long may Willamette's valley smile in peace,
Her labors lessening as her fruits increase.
Here the dread sounds of war have never come,
To tear the husband from his much-loved home ;

To rend the maiden's heart, as to the strife
Her lover goes, to offer up his life.
Oh, may no eye of those assembled here
Be doomed to shed the unavailing tear
For dear ones, lost beneath the surging wave
Of War, that dots our land with many a grave !

And now, farewell ! the dearest friends must part,
Although the breast may throb, the tear-drop start.
And when far, far from you my lot is cast,
Think not that aught can ever blot the past.
No ! faithful to the hearts that met me here,
And strewed my path with flowers of sweetest
      cheer,
Memory will turn, when clouds obscure my way,
To find in thoughts of you a brighter day.
Fain would I linger here, but voices come
On every breeze, to whisper of my home ;
My home ! where fond ones wait with tearful eye,
And watch each sail that looms against the sky.
Yes, though the tear-drop start, the bosom swell,
I must, regretful, speak the sad Farewell !

3

TO ADDIE.

Joyous smiles and tears of sadness
  Mingle round our hearth to-day,
Where the blissful tones of gladness
  Have been fondly prone to stay.
She, our loved one, with another
  Goes, the path of life to share,
Leaving dear ones, father, mother,
  Sad, with one more vacant chair.

Oh, my precious one, my daughter!
  "Oh, my winsome Adelaide!"
Winsome from the days of childhood,
  When between our knees you prayed;
Can the heart you now have chosen
  Beat with love for you like ours?
Must the parent-love be frozen,
  Gazing on these nuptial flowers?

One short year has scarcely wasted
  Since your darling sister left,

Then the pangs of grief we tasted,
 Now again are we bereft!
Who shall now that bright smile bring us?
 Who restore those sounds of mirth?
Who shall now the old songs sing us,
 As we watch our lonely hearth?

Yet we know that thou art happy,
 And, though we may meet no more,
We shall not forget the meeting
 Promised on the farther shore!
Earth affords no joy, no laughter,
 But some bleeding hearts are nigh,
Waiting for the great Hereafter
 In God's glorious by and by!

So our sad farewell is spoken,
 And we press that darling form,
Though our heart-strings, wrung and broken,
 Seem like wrecks amid the storm!
Good-by, Addie! Lips no fonder
 Ever pressed a daughter's brow;
Oh, where'er through life you wander,
 Think of home, so lonely now!

January 22, 1879.

EASTER HYMN.

WRITTEN FOR ZION PROTESTANT EPISCOPAL CHURCH, NEW-
PORT, R. I., EASTER SUNDAY, 1877.

HARK, the joyful carol sounding
　From the ransomed, far and wide!
Faithful hearts with joy are bounding,
　Praising Him, the Crucified!
Banish now all tones of sadness,
　Bring fresh flowers to strew his way,
Let our mourning turn to gladness,
　" Christ the Lord is risen to-day!"

God Incarnate soars to heaven,
　Pleads his wounds and sufferings here,
Precious price of sin forgiven,
　Wounds that bring redemption near!
Angels bright repeat the story,
　While glad hosts, in white array,
Join our Easter song of glory,
　" Christ the Lord is risen to-day!"

Ho, redeemed ones! Chant his praises!
Let new songs declare your joy;
Lo, the pall of darkness raises,
Sin and sorrow to destroy!
Death hath flown, and life immortal
Cheers us on our glorious way
To Jerusalem's blest portal,
"*Christ our Lord is risen to-day!*"

May our hearts with fond devotion
Keep the promise ever nigh,
Till we reach that blissful ocean,
In the glorious by and by!
May no earthly prospect please us,
Till on wings we soar away,
There to sing the songs of Jesus
Christ our Lord, through endless day!

POETIC ADDRESS.

WRITTEN FOR THE CELEBRATION OF ST. JOHN THE
BAPTIST'S DAY.

HAIL, mystic brothers! Favored sons of Light,
Who come together on this festive night,
To worship the Grand Architect of heaven,
And ask that blessing may be freely given
To all who dwell upon this fleeting earth,
Whether in hovel or in halls of mirth, —
Thrice welcome all! On this proud natal day,
SAINT JOHN THE BAPTIST guides us on our way,
While forms of beauty gather here to-night,
To cheer us on with smiles and glances bright!

Religion's handmaid — glorious Masonry!
Ennobling those who truly follow thee, —
What notes can chant thy praises, or declare
The joys and virtues thy true followers share.

Behold the Mason as he first explores
The hidden depths within our mystic doors;

He leaves his helpless state, and from the night
Of darkness enters on a blaze of light.
Behold him, as with firm though bated breath, —
His agonies resembling those of death, —
He enters boldly on the task to prove
The wondrous merits of MASONIC LOVE!
Here first he stands with opened eyes, to be
A model of true worth and secrecy;
Here is revealed to his astonished sight
The awful grandeur of "LET THERE BE LIGHT!"
And here he learns that in the Mason's school
The HOLY BIBLE is the only rule.
The Square and Compasses are held to view
As curbing his desires and passions too.
Clothed with the lamb-skin as his sure defense,
Emblem of purity and innocence,
He in the North-East corner takes his place,
The youngest Mason, full of new found grace.
Perfect and upright Mason, there he stands,
The gauge and gavel in his worthy hands,
While, over all, the starry blue expanse
Spreads, the anticipation to enhance,
Of that good time for which all Masons strive,
When in the Lodge above they shall arrive,
By Jacob's ladder, whose three rounds so fair,
Faith, Hope, and Charity, shall guide them there.

He learns to meet upon the Level too,
To act upon the Plumb as brother true,
And, when his lodge from labor doth repair,
He learns to part with brethren on the Square.
His guiding rules, all handed from above,
Relief and Truth joined with a brother's Love,
Temperance, Fortitude, and Prudence too,
With solid Justice, form his system true!

Behold him further on, progressing still,
And climbing slowly the Masonic hill.
The Plumb, the Square, the Level still appear
As guides upon his mystical career;
Between the brazen pillars he attends,
And with his guide the winding stairs ascends
Into that chamber where fresh light is gained,
And where the liberal arts are all explained.
Here to the heights of science he can soar,
Set forth in language never heard before.
The sheaf of wheat, the waterfall, are taught,
New rays of light are to his vision brought, —
Till his dazed eyes are opened wide to see
The hidden meaning of the letter G!

But the sublime for him is yet to dawn;
Behold him as he travels further on.

SANCTUM SANCTORUM he has gained at last,
And through the TEMPLE-BUILDER'S trials
     passed !
Faithful and true, with firm Masonic nerve,
Death fails to force him from his vows to
     swerve !
Rather the torture, rather dust to dust,
Than shirk his duty or betray his trust !
Here we behold the perfect man, imbued
With all the graces of our brotherhood ;
Triumphing over death, firm fixed is he
In hope of glorious Immortality !
Such is our noble brotherhood, — and still
The sad events near Mount Moriah's hill
And at the Temple Gates must e'er remain
Impressed upon our hearts while Time shall
     reign !

What is the Mason's mission ? 'T is no less
Than to relieve a brother in distress, —
To heal the widow's woes, to soothe her sigh,
And dry the tear from the poor orphan's eye !
To keep inviolate the holy vow
Of universal friendship, and to bow
Before the shrine of Him who gives us grace
To frame our hearts fit for His dwelling-place ;

Who watches o'er our work, and deigns to be
Our Teacher in all acts of purity.
Brethren, it is for this we meet and part,
And serve with hand to hand and heart to
        heart.
The world our Lodge, we seek ourselves to
        raise
To that grand sphere where reigns the King of
        Days,
And there through an eternity of youth
Drink from the fountain of Jehovah's Truth!

Let us our mission ever keep in sight, —
And, as we leave this sacred house to-night,
Let us remember that great truth we teach,
That we are surely traveling on to reach
"That undiscovered country, from whose bourn
No traveler is e'er permitted to return;"
And that our loved ACACIA blooms to prove
The endless ages of Almighty Love, —
Pointing us to those glorious realms on high,
Where souls redeemed can never, never die.

GENERAL TAYLOR

OLD ZACHARY the brave
Was preparing to shave,
And had just taken off his bandanna;
His beard long and gray
Had grown since the day
He had peppered the proud Santa Anna!

A courier from home,
Steed covered with foam,
Arrived with the latest newspaper, —
The razor was dropped
And the General popped
Out, to read by the light of a taper.

His eye met the top —
He the paper let drop —
His cheek first turned red, and then paler,
For there stood to view,
And in capitals too,
"FOR PRESIDENT, GENERAL TAYLOR!"

He called Major Bliss —
"Here, by Jove ! look at this !
I 'll soon stop it I 'll lay them a wager !
For me to aspire !
Why death and h—l-fire !
You know that I never did, Major ! "

" I 've rode myself sore
To get through this d—d war,
Although I 've had poor transportation ;
And all that I do
Has one object in view —
To conquer a peace for the Nation ! "

" And Major, I swear
I don't think it fair,
In spite of the pains I am taking,
To be talking before
I have finished this war,
Of elections and President-making ! "

So saying, he went
On his shaving intent,
But 't was nothing but ripping and tearing !
And the last that we saw
He had Bragg by the paw,
And Lord ! how the General was swearing !

MY OLD KNAPSACK.

FARE THEE WELL, my good old knapsack!
  I must part with thee at last;
Since I took thee as companion
  We have weathered many a blast;
Through the Palo Alto thunder
  And Resaca's field of blood,
Thou has faced it out, old fellow,
  And unscathed in battle stood!

When dark night had closed the carnage
  Of that great victorious day,
And I slept in mud so weary
  In the fort at Monterey, —
Dead companions all around me
  In that dark and bloody den, —
Then I found thy worth, old knapsack:
  How I owned thy virtues then!

Vera Cruz and Cerro Gordo
  Each have tried thy sinews well;

Stern Contreras — Churubusco —
　All thy many virtues tell.
Firm Chapultepec beheld thee
　Ere it met its overthrow,
And thy march with me was onward
　Till unslung in Mexico.

Thou wert ever true, old fellow,
　Thou to me wert ever true;
I have carried thee in summer,
　And when Texan northers blew;
When my friends had all deserted,
　When my foes looked doubly black,
When fond hope had almost yielded,
　Still I found thee at my back!

How my tears have coursed adown thee,
　Pillowed on the desert sand,
As I read my mother's letters,
　Penned with aged trembling hand,
Or perused a sister's missive,
　Breathing o'er me childhood's spell,
Calling home the wayward wanderer,
　Let the chords of memory tell!

When with pain my head was throbbing,
　And fatigued and worn I lay,

Thinking of the morrow's conflict,
  And of loved ones far away,
Weary, heart-sick, sad, and foot-sore,
  Dark seemed all the world to me,
'Reft of all save thee, old knapsack,
  Could I fail of loving thee?

True, I little thought, old fellow,
  When I shouldered thee at first,
That the *ties* which bound so firmly,
  All were doomed in time to burst;
But alas! thy coat is threadbare,
  "Where my head so oft hath lain,"
And the care once lavished on thee
  Ne'er can be bestowed again!

And when I, worn out in service,
  'Neath the sod shall be laid down,
When no more the front of battle
  Shall inspire me with its frown,
May some noble-hearted comrade,
  Kindly, to my memory,
Shed an honest tear, old knapsack,
  As is falling now for thee.

VERA CRUZ, MEXICO, *January* 20, 1848.

TO THE TORN FLAG, THIRD UNITED STATES INFANTRY.

WAVE ON, proud flag! Wave on,
  Nor blush to own the scars
So proudly, nobly won
  Amid the din of wars!
Thy willing folds shake out,
  Well pierced although they be,
In the Resaca's rout
  They led to victory!

Wave on, to tell the foe
  Thy Stars are on the way
To shine in Mexico
  Bright as at Monterey!
Speak out in glorious might;
  Tell them the fierce onset
Of Cerro Gordo's height
  Is but a foretaste yet!

Well hast thou made us feel
  That, foremost in the fight,

Thy presence nerves the steel
 That strikes for freedom's right !
That shattered as thou art,
 Torn though thy foldings be,
The sight still cheers the heart
 And bids us on with thee !

April 20, 1847.

4

RESACA DE LA PALMA.

WITH our own proud eagle's flight,
And with armor flashing bright,
To defend a Nation's right
    Did we come ;
Every heart was beating high,
While the flashing of each eye
Told that all would freely die
    For our home !

On the Rio Bravo's stream
Did our brightened sabres gleam,
And our thoughts as in a dream
    Float before us,
As we wandered hours and hours
To gaze upon thy towers,
Rising out from groves of flowers,
    Matamoros !

But, alas! the tale to tell :
From the tangled chaparral,

Where brave Cross and Porter fell
     Rose the cry,
As each warrior seized his gun
And for vengeance swiftly run
For the bloody murders done,
     Or to die !

See our gallant veterans close
As the shouts so wildly rose,
And we dashed upon our foes,
     Each brave band !
Tremble, Mexico ! The hour
To assert a Nation's power
And deal a righteous dower
     Is at hand !

Now we reap the vengeance due !
See ! their ranks are falling through —
While their stiffening corses strew
     Every spot !
See the gore in streamlets gush,
As their vanquished thousands rush
For the river, through the brush !
     Halt them not !

Let them cross to whence they came,
And if glory's torch of flame

Is not smothered by their shame ;
　　If their scars
　Still incite when battle calls ;
　Though many a warrior falls
　We 'll in Montezuma's halls
　　Plant the Stars !

FAREWELL TO MEXICO.

WRITTEN ON EMBARKING FROM VERA CRUZ, MEXICO, JAN-
UARY, 1848.

FAIR Land, at length I leave thee ; yet
   Thy silvery streams and sunny skies
Fade from my view without regret,
   With not a tear to dim these eyes.
I leave thy mountains crowned with snow,
   Thy temples with their marble floors,
Where kneels the maid whose whisper low
   In humble suppliance heavenward soars.
      No more my footsteps o'er thee roam,
      A voice superior calls me home !

I 've wandered o'er thy flowery fields,
   And pensive sat beside thy streams ;
I 've owned the power which beauty wields,
   In daylight thoughts, in midnight dreams ;
Yes, I have loved an Aztec maid,
   Her listening ear has heard my sighs,

And oh ! I could have always stayed
  To gaze into those dark, dark eyes,
    But that my own paternal dome
    Looms up to call the wanderer home.

I 've seen thy choicest warriors fall
  Before the rifles' deadly aim,
And mourned thy millions held in thrall
  By fiends who seek inglorious fame ;
I 've seen the comrades at my side
  Amid the cheers of victory die,
And laughed, aye, shouted, in my pride
  To see thy rent battalions fly !
    But, blood enough ; I cross the foam
    To greet once more my own dear home.

Farewell ! I leave thee not alone,
  The Stars and Stripes still proudly deck
Thy palaces of massive stone,
  Thy lofty towers, Chapultepec ;
I leave thee, all fond thoughts repressing,
  All bright and sunny as thou art,
I go to meet a parent's blessing,
  And glad once more a sister's heart.
    A thousand breezes sweetly come
    To waft me to my childhood's home.

TO MY OLD MUSKET.

GOOD-BY, old musket mine, good-by !
I leave thee not without a sigh,
For many a year we 've passed together,
In sunshine and in stormy weather ;
   And though the parting wrings my heart,
   Yet, dear old comrade, we must part.

Oh, many a wet and weary way,
Through the dark swamps of Florida,
With aching limbs and blistered feet,
I 've tramped, the Seminole to meet ;
   And many a night in bivouac lay,
   And hugged thee in my arms till day.

On Palo Alto's well-fought field
The dread artillery thunder pealed,
And though thy tones were heard not then,
Nor foeman stood within thy ken,
   I felt the love which war reveals
   The warrior for his musket feels.

Resaca de la Palma heard
The voice of war within thee stirred ;
And when we paused, with victory crowned,
Wounded and dying strewed around,
  I held thee closer to my heart,
  For thou hadst nobly done thy part.

Still on, old friend, through smoke and blood,
At Monterey we stoutly stood ;
Dread Vera Cruz we saw laid low
In spite of sullen, desperate foe ;
  And Cerro Gordo's bristling height
  We reached in thickest of the fight.

Ah, shall I e'er forget the morn
I bore thee through the waving corn,
As down the slope we proudly rushed
Where Padierna's [1] hosts were crushed?
  Thy stock was shivered by a blow,
  But I was safe — forget it ? No !

Shall I forget that same proud day,
When, hot for Churubusco's fray,
I knelt upon the blood-stained sward
And strengthened thee with scanty cord,

[1] Contreras.

Then with a shout of victory soon
Rushed on to join our brave platoon?

Good-by, old musket mine! Thy lock
Hath weathered many a tempest-shock!
And though I leave thee with regret,
And go to don the epaulette,
  It never shall forgotten be
  That epaulette was won through thee!

THE PARTING AT FORT SUMTER.

THE fog around Fort Sumter
  Was drifting fast away,
When through the mist a schooner
  Sailed slowly down the bay;
No union flag she boasted,
  Star emblem of the free,
But fore and aft there floated
  The lone Palmetto tree.

Fond hearts were sadly beating
  Within that strong-walled fort,
For wives and children waited
  Without the sally-port, —
Waited in mournful silence
  The signal to depart,
Which shook with throes of anguish
  Each wife's and mother's heart.

" Arrah, Norah! don't be cryin'!"
  A Celtic soldier spoke,
" Sure we 'll never think of dyin'
  Till the last stale biscuit 's broke.

And, darlin', trust the Major,
　He 'll bring us right at last ! "
But vain the attempt at soothing,
　The tears fell hot and fast.

" It 's not for that, my husband,
　It 's not for fear I weep,
I know the gallant Major
　Your lives will safely keep ;
It 's for the cruel mandate
　That hurries me away,
Because a coward President
　Would starve you if I stay ! "

" I know the Nation 's watching
　The gallant Major's course,
And countless hearts are yearning
　To aid his little force ;
But prayers will never feed you,
　Nor send more men to fight,
Though this sad parting gives you
　One biscuit more to-night ! "

" Walter, my son, my first-born,
　Though I must leave you now,
Think of this kiss at parting
　I 'm sealing on your brow ;

And if the rage of battle
  Should chance to lay you low,
Your life 's your country's, Walter,
  Your brother's ended so."

But see, the boat is nearing,
  And in the distance, too,
Crowds throng the Charleston levee
  To cheer the parting few.
"Good-by, love!" "Good-by, darling!"
  And manly hearts are pressed
With tearful, sad devotion
  To many a loved one's breast!

The fog around Fort Sumter
  Had drifted far away;
A trim and gallant schooner
  Sailed swiftly from the Bay;
Eyes watched her from the ramparts,
  That trim and gallant sail,
As from her deck there floated
  Fond woman's mournful wail!

Eyes watched her from the ramparts
  All wet with manly tears,
Wrung from the soul's affection,
  Not from unmanly fears;

But, as the white speck faded,
  Up rose those sons of war:
"Three cheers for -Major Anderson!
  Huzza! Huzza!! Huzza!!!"

NATIONAL HYMN.

HOME of the free-born! Happy land!
   Where man, progressive, proud, and free,
In God-like majesty doth stand,
   Full type of human liberty:
Land of our love! Thy banner bright
   Lights up with joy the patriot's eye;
Beneath its folds thy sons unite,
   For thee to live, or nobly die!

Land of the glorious Washington!
   Who broke the haughty tyrant's chain,
And led our sires to victories, won
   A priceless heritage to gain;
Hail to thy Stars! Let each fair breeze
   Kiss that bright flag, whose folds, elate,
Shall wave through unborn centuries
   On every tower, in every State!

Oh, may the arm of God delay —
   Should section still with section strive —

The horrors of that direful day
　When War our liberties may rive!
May Peace and Plenty yet abound,
　And wholesome counsel ne'er depart;
And may our Union still be found
　First, dearest to each patriot heart.

Long may our much-loved banner float,
　With every star intact and bright,
Blest cynosure to climes remote,
　Whose millions hail its glittering light!
Long may our emblem-eagle's wing
　Its peaceful shelter mildly spread,
While new-born nations gladly sing
　Their resurrection from the dead!

Home of the free-born! Happy land!
　Where man, progressive, proud, and free,
In God-like majesty doth stand,
　Full type of human liberty.
Land of our love! Thy banner bright
　Lights up with joy the patriot's eye;
Beneath its folds thy sons unite,
　For thee to live, or nobly die!

April, 1865.

"MISSING."

WHEN will you come back again, papa,
    To sit in the old arm-chair,
And read the Bible to mother and me,
    And join in our evening prayer?
Oh, you dear, you cruel papa,
    If you knew how we grieve to-night,
Would n't you leave that hateful war
    And come to your home so bright?

When will he come back again, mamma?
    I only wish I could read
That letter you moisten so with tears, —
    But my prattle you scarcely heed.
Soldiers in crowds are passing by,
    As I gaze down the lighted street,
And I long to ask them about papa,
    As they hurry their friends to greet.

Don't you remember the day, mamma,
    When the news from Fort Sumter came,
That the gallant old Major Anderson
    Had won such a glorious name?

When papa wore such a bright, bright sword
  At the head of his company?
And how proud we felt as he marched along,
  When he smiled on you and me?

Don't you remember the words he said
  When he kissed us the night before,
And sat on the side of my little bed,
  To tell me about the war?
How can I ever forget his look,
  As he mournfully said to you,
" Dear, dear Nellie, I love you both,
  But I love the Union too!

" Nellie, when on the battle-field
  I share in the conflict wild,
I shall be thinking of you alone —
  You and our darling child.
Wherever our Union banner floats
  There will my station be,
Till the rebel hordes are in full retreat
  From the field of victory!"

Yes, and he promised to write, mamma,
  But only one letter came;

5

Why don't he write to his little girl,
    If only to write my name?
How he would grieve if he knew you cried
    And looked at his picture so!
Surely, oh, surely he'd hasten home
    With the crowd that is passing now.

As they pass the door to-night, mamma,
    They whisper the name " Bull Run ; "
Is that the name of a battle-field?
    Have the Union soldiers won?
They pass along with a saddened look,
    Their voices are hoarse and low,
It was not thus when they marched away,
    Two or three months ago!

Don't let me make you cry, mamma,
    My tears are all dried and gone,
Now I must say my little prayers,
    And sleep till the morning dawn.
God in heaven! look down to-night,
    Watch over our father dear ;
Shelter him in the stormy fight,
    And pilot him safely here!

Ah, you cruel, you dear papa,
    If you knew how we grieve to-night,

Would n't you leave the battle-field
  And come to your home so bright?
When will you come back again, papa,
  To sit in the old arm-chair,
And read the Bible at night once more,
  And join in our evening prayer?

August, 1861.

DECORATION DAY.

THE MOTHER.

THEY deck with flowers thy grave, my noble
    boy,
  On this the holiest day of all the year;
My grateful heart leaps with a thrill of joy
  That bids me strive to check the rising tear.

This is my hour of pride, my warrior son!
  I give thy grave up to thy country's care,
To those who, ere their mournful task is done,
  Will strew that mound with flowers all sweet
    and rare.

My day of pride! A mother's heart beats high
  To know thou 'rt numbered with that gallant
    band
Who sought the glorious privilege to die,
  With arms and face to foe, for our dear land!

Tears I have shed for thee, my soldier child,
   Nor ceased my weeping since that parting
      day,
When the closed patriot phalanx onward filed
   To meet the foe, and crush his proud array.

But for to-day no weeping! Not one tear
   Shall down this pale and wasted cheek be
      borne!
A nation decks thy grave, and thousands here
   Assemble, o'er the gallant dead to mourn.

Yes, let that nation weep! Enough for me,
   To-day, that thou art of the honored ones;
To know that thus, for centuries yet to be,
   The nation's heart will throb for these lost
      sons!

Enough for me to know that our great chief,
   Who brought his hosts victorious from the
      fray,
Joins, with a full heart in the signs of grief,
   These honors to our Union dead to-day.

And so to-day no tears! But oh, my brave!
   To-morrow, when the mournful pageant's o'er,

Shall I not visit thy untimely grave,
  Dear boy, and wet it with my tears once
  more?

Yes, and my harrowing· grief may then have
  vent,
  Unshared, unnoticed by to-day's sad crowd,
And a 'reft mother's sobs, now bravely pent,
  May fill the air with grief-tones long and
  loud.

Till then, farewell, my lost, my warrior son!
  Till then I leave thy grave thy country's care,
And generous hands will, ere the day is done,
  Bedeck that mound with flowers all sweet and
  rare.

TRIBUTE TO THE MEMORY OF MAJOR-GENERAL FRED. STEELE, U. S. A.

WELL may a comrade's tear-drop start,
Thou veteran of the noble heart,
   At bidding thee farewell;
Hero of many a stirring fight!
What pen thine epitaph shall write, —
   Thy manly virtues tell ?

The lion-heart, the undefiled
And gentle nature of a child
   Were blent within that breast;
The faithful friend, the bitter foe,
Who spurned the action mean or low —
   Thou wert by all confessed !

The smile deceitful won thee not;
The frown no impress on thee wrought;
   Thou wast not born to crouch :
Candid to foe, to friend sincere,
We knew thee as the chevalier
   " *Sans peur, et sans reproche !* "

We marked thee in Contreras' fray,
In Churubusco's hard-fought day,
   And red Molino's fight;
And 'mid the blood and smoke and wreck
Of towering, proud Chapultepec
   Thy blade was flashing bright!

Missouri's fields thy prowess tell,
And where th' undaunted Lyon fell
   Thy sword was seen to wave;
And History's page will fondly speak
Of valorous deeds at Wilson's Creek,
   A Nation's life to save.

Vicksburg's all-glorious scenes of war,
The struggles on Arkansas' shore,
   Close up the record grand;
And sadly falls the soldier's tear,
As round the flag-enshrouded bier
   Thy sorrowing comrades stand!

And this the epitaph they write,
In letters gemmed with living light,
   To deck thy funeral pile : —
" *Here lies Fred. Steele, a chieftain brave;*
Tread lightly o'er a warrior's grave,
   Who knew nor fear nor guile! "

POEM

DELIVERED AT THE BROWNSVILLE NATIONAL CEMETERY,
TEXAS, ON DECORATION DAY, MAY 31, 1880.

WE stand upon this holy ground to-day,
With one accord a sacred debt to pay ;
To offer honors to the gallant dead,
And strew with flowers the warriors' lowly bed.
Not with draped colors nor with muffled drum,
Not with the notes of mourning do we come ;
These, though the signs of woe, are soon forgot,
So not with these we greet this grassy spot.
We come with hearts elate, bright flowers to
      spread,
And tribute pay to our illustrious dead.
Our soldiers and our sailors buried here
Demand these sacred rites from year to year.

I see around me veterans worn and gray,
Who bear the scars of many a desperate fray :
Some dealt beneath the flag of Single Star,
When Texas braved alone the brunt of war ;

Some on the torrid plains of Mexico,
And some on fields where brethren dealt the
blow.
Widows and orphans, too, assemble here
To strew their flowers and shed the silent tear;
While, adding fitness to the glorious scene,
With forms erect and sternly martial mien,
The soldier and the sailor proudly stand,
The twin protectors of our happy land!

Just nineteen years have rolled their months
away
Since gathering armies mustered for the fray;
Then the land trembled with a Nation's tramp,
And North, South, East, and West were one vast
camp.
The deadly conflict, rife with blood and tears,
Raged in its might through four long frightful
years,
When carnage ceased, and Peace resumed her
reign,
And the worn warriors sought their homes again.
But ah! how many thousands vainly look
For dear ones, who for war their homes for-
sook, —
For husbands, fathers, sons and brothers dear,

Whose loving smiles no more shall greet them
    here.
Some on the battle-fields unsheltered lie,
Dead in their gore, their covering the sky ;
While other thousands slept beneath the sands,
After rough burial at their comrades' hands.

From many a hard-fought field the sad remains
Are gathered to these homes, where silence reigns,
And kind and faithful hands have laid them
    where
True friends and patriots annually repair
To deck with flowers each gallant soldier's grave,
Who died with face to foe, our land to save !

Some of these head-stones do not bear a name,
To speak to future age the soldier's fame ;
The Grand Division of the brave "*unknown*"
Rest in their graves crowned by a nameless stone !
But while to-day we gladly gather here,
To honor *all* these heroes with a tear,
We only care to know they marched and fought,
Through blood and fire our priceless victories
    wrought,
And offered up their lives in cause so dear
To you, to me, to all assembled here !

Some by the murderous bullet bravely fell ;
Some, lingering, died beneath the fever's spell.
Yes ! sorrowing mothers, wives and sisters too,
We come to honor those so dear to you !
What though their names deck no funereal stone,
There is a region bright where *all are known*,
And where the brave who rest beneath the sod
In spirit roam, in the full light of God !

And was this precious blood poured out in vain ?
Was it for nought we gave these martyred slain ?
Behold the Stars and Stripes in peaceful sway !
From gulf to lake no bondman bows to-day !
From these great sacrifices we have gained
A nation newly born, a race unchained !
Hark to the song, 't is Freedom's glorious strain,
And franchised millions swell the glad refrain !

We stand to-day among the graves of some
Who rallied at the sound of Southern drum.
We come not here to single out their graves, —
Let it suffice that these were also braves !
They were our brethren, and they bravely fought
To guard the doctrines from their childhood
        taught ;
And patriot hearts will not withhold their due,
As here they sleep, *the gray beside the blue !*

Here also is the grave of many a one
Who came to die beneath this Southern sun.
On Palo Alto's plain they met the foe,
And braved the marshaled hosts of Mexico.
Some in Resaca's charge were stricken down,
Some slain amid the thunders of Fort Brown!
All honor to these noble sons of war,
Who left their homes to succor the Lone Star!
From North and South, from East and West, they
      came,
That little band, and won a glorious name!

Here lies brave Jacob Brown, whose name shall
      stand
A watchword on the winding Rio Grande,
While deeds of valor deck the roll of Fame,
And Brownsville bears his grand historic name!
The names of Ringgold, Chadbourne, Page, and
      Blake,
Inge, Cochrane, Stevens too, shall live to wake
Within the hearts of warriors yet to be,
The spirit that leads on to victory!
The spirit that bore Zachary Taylor on
Till Buenavista's field was reached and won!

Yes, comrades, friends, let us from year to year
Come from our homes to lay our offerings here, —

Come with our sons, our daughters, and our wives,
To visit those who offered up their lives ;
Thus nursing in our hearts that fealty true
To home and country ever justly due,
By honoring those laid in their narrow beds,
Who bore that flag now waving o'er our heads !

THE OLD SUPERINTENDENT OF NATIONAL CEMETERY.

"Four hundred thousand men,
   The good, the brave, the true,
On battle plain, in prison pen,
   Lie dead for me and you !
Four hundred thousand of the brave
Have made our ransomed soil their grave,
   For me and you !
Good friend, for me and you ! "

Yes, sir, I 'm the Superintendent ; walk in, please,
   and have a chair —
There 's a heavy fog this morning, and it sort o'
   chills the air ;
But the sun is breaking through it, and I reckon
   we may say
That we 're going to have a beauty this thirtieth
   of May.
The lodge ? Why yes, it 's cosy and comfortable
   enough
For an old and broken soldier who is used to
   takin' it rough ;

And the quartermaster-general does all that can be
    done
To fix us — and why would n't he? the war cost
    him a son.

My Army? Yes, Lord bless you! why here they
    lie in rows,
And I know each soldier's name by heart, as far
    as naming goes;
That dozen rows out yonder, where you see that
    pile of stone,
Is the left flank of my army — the brigade of the
    " *Unknown!* "
But they 'll get their share of flowers in the strew-
    ing of to-day,
And you 'll see some wet eyelashes there this
    thirtieth day of May:
For the Nation's heart claims all of them on this
    proud day of ours,
And it does n't take a fancy name to fetch the
    tears and flowers!

Long service? Well, I 've had my share, and forty
    years ago
I hunted in the everglades to catch the Indian
    foe;

I fought at Okee-cho-bee in old " Rough and
    Ready's " band,
And bore my knapsack many a day through Flor-
    ida's burning sand.
On the field of Palo Alto, at Resaca, too, I fought,
Where the loss of noble fellows made our victories
    dearly bought ;
In Taylor's ranks at Monterey I met Ampudia's
    crew,
Where the *Third* went in three hundred and came
    out seventy-two !

Yes, Grant was there, on every field he met the
    tawny foe,
From the fight at Palo Alto to the halt in Mexico ;
And the boys of our brigade took heart, as to the
    front they ran,
At the words of cheer that met them from that
    young and gallant man !
They tell me he 's not changed a bit since he 's
    the Nation's Head,
And I know that he 'll not soon forget our noble
    Union dead ;
For I heard that last year in the storm, the thir-
    tieth of May,
He joined the throng at Arlington on Decoration
    Day.
    6

Do I find it lonesome? No, sir; I sit for many
　　a night
At the foot of that old flagstaff, when the moon is
　　shining bright,
And the wind is whistling hoarsely, and the rush-
　　ing of the blast
Makes the halyards flap a tattoo against the tow-
　　ering mast;
And my memory gathers round me all the com-
　　rades brave I knew,
From Bull Run to Appomattox, — now reposing
　　'neath the dew;
Then I fall asleep and dream of these, my com-
　　rades with the dead,
Till I waken with the chilliness and totter off to
　　bed.

Then it makes up for the loneliness, this thirtieth
　　day of May,
When I meet with some good faces I have met
　　here many a day;
Fathers, mothers, sisters, brothers, weeping friends
　　who gladly come
To scatter Spring's bright flowers o'er their lost
　　ones' early tomb!

Ah ! it makes my old frame tremble when I see
    the falling tear
From eyes that speak the love that brings the
    annual pilgrims here ;
And when some stricken mother vents her grief
    in accents low,
Then I 'm hurried back to childhood — ah, God !
    that 's long ago !

They tell me that the fair ones of the South will
    strew their flowers
When next they hold " Memorial Day," on both
    their graves and *ours ;*
Well, this is right ; I 'm glad to see good feeling
    coming round,
For hatred never moved the boys who lie beneath
    the ground.
Look ! over in that corner sleep a dozen " *boys
    in gray,*"
And I twine a wreath for each of them on Dec-
    oration Day !
For who shall judge the hearts of those that grassy
    mound conceals ?
We 've had our fight and bear no grudge — that 's
    how a soldier feels !

I 'm looking forward, knowing that when I 'm dead
    and gone,
And in one of these neat grassy rows they plant
    the usual stone,
Some lover of the soldier will, with kind and faith-
    ful hand,
Drop roses on the grave of one who fought to
    save the land !
Well, I see the crowd is coming, so we 'll step
    out, if you please,
That 's my bench, there in the shadow of those
    two tall willow trees ;
There 's my crutches ; thank you kindly ; you may
    help me o'er the sill.
Sir ? my leg ? oh, that lies buried at the foot of
    Malvern Hill !

    May, 1873.

THE VETERAN OF THE MEXICAN WAR.

HALT there, veteran! for I know you by the
    badge that decks your breast!
Listen, while I faintly picture how a soldier of
    the West
Fought and died for our loved country, — paying
    thus the patriot's debt, —
Braved the hordes of Santa Anna, and the mur-
    derous escopet!
Many a brave boy left his mother for the fields
    of Mexico,
Whose white bones are bleaching whiter near the
    mountains tipped with snow;
Many a brother left a sister, many a true heart
    left his love, —
Left, no more to clasp the dear ones till they
    meet in courts above!
You are spared to tell the story, you are here to
    join the ranks
Of those worn and shattered veterans who receive
    the Nation's thanks!

Though your sleeve to-day be empty, though all
    pensionless you stand
With the crowds that come to hail the great Cen-
    tennial of our land,
Yet cheer up ! for day is breaking, and the coun-
    try's heart to-day
Beats with gratitude, and greets you as when
    freshest from the fray !
List, then, to your comrade's story, told to loving
    ones whose hands
Bathed his temples, smoothed his pillow, as he
    passed to heavenly lands ;
See him, languishing and wounded, in his West-
    ern home to die ;
Hear him tell of glorious battles fought where
    mountains pierce the sky.

. . . .

" I 'm faint, but oh, how happy now !
    There, let me lean upon your breast,
  It cools the fever on my brow
    To know I am once more at rest ;

" Come nearer, sister ; take my hand,
    I feel death slowly stealing on ;
  Nearer, I 'll tell thee of that band
    That many a gallant field has won.

" I need not speak the joy I felt
  When first the summons called ' to arms ! '
My trusty sword, my warrior belt,
  Had each to me a thousand charms ;

" Nor how, when marshaled with our host,
  I glanced along the serried line,
And felt that I could truly boast
  It held no sturdier form than mine.

" On Palo Alto's well-fought field
  We first stood forth to meet the foe,
The veteran Taylor seized the rein
  That curbed the pride of Mexico.

" Like grass before the scythe we mowed them ;
  Our well-trained coursers trod the field,
As if they knew the hearts that rode them
  Were there to conquer, not to yield !

" With souls as firm and nerves as steady
  As ancient Sparta's sons possessed,
We rallied round ' Old Rough and Ready,'
  And victory perched on every crest.

" E'en now, while I relate the story,
  My sinking spirit seems more light,

For there the first bright glimpse of glory
Rolled up before my ravished sight.

"Ringgold and Duncan from our flanks
Covered the field with dead and dying,
Shrapnel and grape tore through their ranks,
And sent their rent battalions flying!

"From noon to dark in smothering smoke
From the rank prairie's burning grasses,
The dread artillery thunder broke,
Nor paused till night obscured the masses.

"Sons of the South, sons of the North,
Fought there as brother shielding brother;
From Maine to Georgia went they forth,
God! may they never fight each other!

. . . .

"Resaca's field next lay before us,
And foes in thousands bit the ground!
Again I joined in victory's chorus,
Again was free from scar or wound.

"Nine thousand escopets were flashing
From the vine-tangled chaparral
Against our nineteen hundred, dashing
Through brush to meet this blaze of hell!

"The hoary veterans of Tampico
  In battery stood, a proud array,
But guns and tumbrils were abandoned
  At Sacket's charge with Charlie May!

"Our glorious Ridgely poured his fire
  In ceaseless volleys through the brush,
Till vanquished, in confusion dire,
  They for the Rio Grandé rush!

"Ah! Rio Bravo, glorious river,
  So smoothly gliding on your way,
May the deep crimson life-drops never
  Color your banks as on that day!

"Ah! Matamoros — clothed in flowers
  Like some fair spot of ancient Spain,
May your darks walls and glittering towers
  Ne'er gaze upon such sight again!
     .   .   .   .
"At Monterey again we met them,
  Intrenched behind their walls of stone,
And though with vigor we beset them,
  Three days and nights they held their own.

"The snow-capped heights of Nuevo Leon
  Heard there the first dread sounds of war,

And many a well-drilled veteran peon
Lay dead, or weltering in his gore.

"Worth, from the Bishop's Palace shelling,
    Sent swift destruction through the town ;
Of Mexique's flower the blood is welling
    Beneath tall Sierra Madre's frown ;

"While Taylor from the eastern plazas,
    His regulars mixed with volunteers,
Tunneled his way straight through the casas,
    And stormed the forts 'mid rousing cheers !

"At length our final charge was sounded ;
    We drove the foe from every gun ;
Though hundreds of brave comrades, wounded,
    Breathed their last sigh ere set of sun.

"Six weeks our brave five thousand rested
    (*Five hundred nobly death had met*) ;
But — '*forward!*' they were to be tested
    On many a field more bloody yet.

.   .   .   .

"At Vera Cruz the blended thunder
    Of friend and foe the sand-hills shook ;
The screeching shells when rent asunder
    Sought out their prey in every nook.

" Each moment proved our arms victorious,
　As day and night Death's errand sped ;
Oh ! 't was a sight sublimely glorious !
　Sister — I faint — raise — raise my head !

" See ! — from our mortar batteries streaming
　The dreadful missiles seek the clouds !
Now hear the crashing, then the screaming,
　As down they plunge on frightened crowds !

" Undaunted Perry from the water
　Batters San Juan de Ulloa's walls ;
Each noble vessel aids the slaughter,
　Till prone the ' Cactus banner ' falls !

" Our veteran Totten never wearies
　Till bursting shell and blazing fuse,
Like eagles swooping from their aeries,
　Complete the doom of Vera Cruz !

　.　　.　　.　　.　　.　　.　　.　　.

" Now onward still, each man a hero,
　We climbed the Cerro Gordo height,
And strewed the fair fields of Encerro
　With hordes who sought inglorious flight !

" Shall I forget the cheers so hearty
　That from the mountain side arose

As Harney led that storming party
  Through showers of grape to meet our foes?

"Up the steep Cerro, hot and flurried,
  Then with clubbed muskets dealing death ;
Then to the swift pursuit we hurried
  With shouts of victory on each breath !

"Here, when the fiery chase had started,
  Led by the proud, impetuous Worth,
A musket ball my bridle parted,
  And horse and rider fell to earth !

"On came the crowd in fury dashing ;
  No power such avalanche could stay ;
I heard the shouts — the sabres clashing ;
  I felt their tread, and swooned away !

"For hours unconscious, crushed and wounded,
  I lay upon that cold earth bed ;
I woke at length, and then there sounded
  An angel whisper near my head.

"I strove to rise and gaze around me, —
  Far off were now the sounds of war ;
Close to the earth my courser bound me, —
  Good steed ! — thou 'lt champ thy bit no more !

"'Stranger, look up; a friend is near thee'"
   (In soft Castilian accent spoken);
"'Within our cot we'll strive to cheer thee,
   And bind thy limbs so bruised and broken.'

"Up to a mountain hut they bore me;
   Long weeks of fever rolled away,
Ere care and kindness could restore me
   To greet once more the light of day.

"My angel nurse, fair Aztec daughter,
   Hung o'er my couch with sweetest care,
And when I feebly called for water,
   The juicy orange still was there!

.   .   .   .

"Upon the rocks at rough Contreras,
   At last I with my comrades stood;
Again the dark-skinned foemen dare us,
   Again begins the work of blood!

"Night fell upon our ranks so steady,
   Fierce rains poured on our weary heads;
But daylight found us bright and ready
   To charge their works through lava beds.

"Forth from the pedregal we drove them;
   That glorious morn I'll ne'er forget;

For death below, and death above them,
  And death on every side they met!

" The gallant Smith to victory led us,
  While veteran Riley followed fast;
And horse and foot in terror fled us,
  As leaves before the Northern blast!

" All flushed with victory and undaunted
  We breasted Churubusco's fire,
And the ' Old Third ' its colors planted
  High on the convent's topmost spire!

"With shouts we crossed the convent ditches
  'Mid raking fire of shot and shell,
Crawling through smoke and crumbling breaches,
  Till wounded, wet with gore, I fell!

" On rode that warrior without tarnish,
  The ever-conquering hero, Scott!
Who in the hour of fire and carnage
  Mercy's sweet promptings ne'er forgot!

" I saw his conscious charger prancing,
  I saw the chieftain's features glow,
And, high o'er all, our flag advancing
  To grace the halls of Mexico!

"Two thousand brave ones, dead and gory,
  Slept tranquil ere the moon arose :
But the eight thousand, crowned with glory,
  Had routed forty thousand foes!

"How Worth's brave cohorts stood the slaughter
  On dark Molino's glorious morn,
When death from escopet and mortar
  Stalked through his ranks so sadly torn ;

"How his stout lads, eleven hundred,
  Lay dead before the fight was done,
While fort and redoubt o'er them thundered
  That day until the field was won ;

"How the proud Capital was taken,
  Its outworks battered to a wreck,
And even the deep foundations shaken
  Of towering, proud Chapultepec, —

"Let others tell ; for faint and bleeding,
  These closing scenes I could not share,
But on my couch, all else unheeding,
  Dreamed of my home and loved ones there!

"Yes, let them tell of Angostura,
  Where Taylor's dwindled force withstood

The shock of Santa Anna's fury,
  And hurled his thousands back subdued !

"Let them recall Taos and Embudo,
  Where our dragoons the onslaught met ;
Where Burgwin fell in glorious battle !
  Where Ingalls won his first brevet !

"You 've asked me, dear ones, '*where 's the glory*'!
  Oh, tell me, have I answered you ?
Have you not heard the stirring story
  Of march, and fight, and victory too ?

"The scattered ranks of proud Arista, —
  The shattered walls of Monterey, —
The slaughtered hosts of Buenavista, —
  Are these not glory, sister, say ?

"Give me some water, I am weary ;
  My tongue is burning, short my breath ;
Oh, for a sleep, the road seems dreary ;
  Quick ! raise me, mother : *is this death ?*

"Ha ! who are these that float around me
  Like pleasant memories of the past ?
What ! Carl ! the faithful friend who found me
  When the life-blood was oozing fast !

"Come nearer, comrade, let me hold you;
  Why thou art cold — whose hand is this?
See, my good Carl, just as I told you,
  I'm home once more: sister, a kiss."

"Carl, my brave heart! dost thou remember
  The rain and mud at Monterey,
That fearful black night in September,
  When we beneath the caissons lay?

"How the 'Black Fort' all night did shell us —
  How as each tour on post was sped,
We crawled, all shivering, to our fellows,
  Mixed up, the living with the dead?

"Dost mind the smoke-wrapped prairie battle,
  Where Mexico's proud crest came down
'Mid iron hail and cannon's rattle, —
  Ha, ha! old Carl, dost mind Fort Brown?

"My brain seems wandering, yet my comrade
  Stood surely at my side; but now
His faithful hand methought was wiping
  This damp that settles on my brow.

"A mist is stealing o'er my senses;
  Ha! now again I'm in the fight,

7

See where tall Harney's charge advances ;
  Look how they poise their bayonets bright !

" I see the scattered legions flying !
  I see the flash of every gun !
O God ! dear mother, this *is* dying ! "

    .   .   .   .

THE WARRIOR SLEEPS — THE VICTORY 'S WON ! "

Thus he passed away, our veteran, home from
    many a weary tramp
From the shores of Corpus Christi to the last
    beleaguered camp !
Let us drop a tear, my comrade ; let us mourn
    with bated breath
· O'er the twenty thousand brave ones in that
    strange land doomed to death !
Land where Grant, the youthful warrior, breasted
    his baptismal fire
On the mountain, in the valley, under many a
    cross-decked spire !
Land that drank the blood of freemen thirty
    long, long years ago ;
Land of silver stream and mountain — thrice un-
    happy Mexico !
But while mourning, still remember that the
    country's heart to-day

Throbs from North to South, and greets you as
    her heroes from the fray !
Though no more the tawny foeman meets you
    on his river banks,
Where the "Northern winged artillery thun-
    dered through his shattered ranks;"
Though your sleeve hang loose and empty, and
    on tottering limbs you stand,
Listening to the great Centennial shout re-
    sounding through the land ;
Let that shout assure you, veteran ; keep your
    banner still unrolled,
For the Nation *will* remember those who won
    the Land of Gold !

TO MINNIE GRACE * * * *

WITH A MORNING-GLORY.

THOU, Minnie, art the Sun, beneath whose rays
We, like the Morning-glories, heed the call ;
While, in thy absence, even our fairest days
Are clothed in sadness like a funeral pall.
But ah, how blest is he who all the while
Enjoys thy rays, and lives within thy smile !

LINES,

WITH A BUNCH OF AUTUMN LEAVES PRESENTED TO MRS.
GENERAL B—— A——.

BROWN Autumn heralds its approach by thee ;
Thy glorious tint on many a leaf appears ;
And thoughts come stealing o'er our hours of
    glee,
Too deep for utterance, yes, too sad for tears.
Oh may our souls, as Summer's bloom we lose,
Be tinted thus with heaven's own Autumn hues !

IMPROMPTU LINES

ON THE DEATH OF PROFESSOR SAMUEL F. B. MORSE. WRITTEN
BY REQUEST ON THE MORNING SUCCEEDING HIS DEATH.

A MIGHTY mind has passed from earth
   To mingle with the glorious throng
Of noble ones who claim their birth
   In this our land of fame and song.
Our Franklin, who the lightning drew;
   Our Fulton, fair Columbia's pride,
Will, with our Morse, their youth renew,
   And view their triumphs side by side!

O hearts that love though seas divide!
   O Nations wrapped in slavery's gloom!
No more the dreary ocean tide
   Can drown your throbs, — pronounce your doom!
The lightning flash that erst with dread
   Inspired each heart, at last appears
To flash with blessings o'er each head, —
   A boon from Heaven, to calm our fears!

Sleep well! oh, casket of a mind
  Too mighty for the earth to hold!
Sleep well! Thy name is left behind
  Written in characters of gold.
And when the last great trump shall sound,
  And all the dead in Christ arise,
That name shall on the roll be found
  Great Victor of the highest prize!

TO A FAIR BUT COLD ONE.

I.

Pleasant in the morning,
  Pleasant still at noon,
Pleasant in the evening
  'Neath the silvery moon;
Pleasant art thou ever
  To my dazzled eyes,
As the glittering iceberg
  Under sunny skies!
Such thou art, and still must be;
Thou the iceberg art to me.

II.

Knowest thou, oh, maiden,
  How I worship thee?
Heedest thou my bosom's
  Fond intensity?
No! thou canst not know it!
  Thou the brooklet art,
Bearing no impression
  On thy placid heart.

Such thou art, so fair to see ;
Thou the brooklet art to me.

III

Gazing in the streamlet
  I behold my face ;
Mirrored on its surface
  Every line I trace ;
Lave my burning forehead ;
  But the ripple there
Scatters all my semblance,
  Leaves me in despair !
Why should I still worship thee ?
Thou the streamlet art to me.

IV.

See the frosted pictures
  On my window pane, —
Trees and ferns and fountains
  Hold their icy reign ;
Brilliant forms and graceful,
  They receive my breath,
And like visions vanish —
  Fade from life to death !
Such art thou, oh, fair to see !
Thou the frost-work art to me.

v.

So I gaze upon thee
  As a distant star
Shining cold and brilliant
  In the ether far;
And thou look'st upon me,
  As the world will soon,
As a petted infant
  Crying for the moon!
Bright and cold thou 'lt ever be;
Ice, brook, frost, star, moon, to me!

THE NIGHT AT MONTEREY.

In the redoubt at Monterey,
  Where many a shell had burst,
Our powder-blackened fellows lay,
  September twenty-first.
All day the battle fierce had raged
  Till this earthwork we won,
And hundreds in the morn engaged
  Lay dead at set of sun.

Night had closed down, and now the rain
  In ceaseless torrents fell,
While from the Black Fort mortar train
  Screeched now and then a shell,
Which, circling o'er the city's length
  In meteoric sport,
Would plunge at last and spend its strength
  In th' ditches of our fort.

Our war-worn boys were scattered round,
  Some on the ramparts lay,
While 'neath the guns, on the wet ground,
  Some tired ones snored away ;
Others more wakeful than the rest
  Oped now and then an eye
To watch the shells, which from the west
  Trailed out across the sky.

My tour on post at two expired,
  To be resumed at six,
And hungry, wet, and very tired,
  (A soldier's common fix !)
Under a caisson, on the ground,
  I reached a muddy bed,
And there a sleeping comrade found
  With blanket-covered head.

I nudged him, but he answered not,
  Then shared his blanket warm ;
I laid awake, and wrapped in thought
  I quite forgot the storm.
Poor boy ! how soundly, silently
  He slept !   How straight each limb !
My God ! I thought, " how glad I'd be
  If I could sleep like him ! "

Day broke ; I heard th' unwelcome shout,
  The warning word, " Relief ! "
I seized my musket and crawled out
  At summons of my chief.
My comrade of the cold, wet bed
  No sign or token gave,
But, stretched beneath the blanket, laid
  As quiet as the grave.

I pull the blanket down, and lo !
  A ghastly, bleeding head,
And rigid, whitened features, show
  Too surely he is dead !
Upon his breast a paper shred
  Torn from a note-book lay,
On which in pencil rough I read
  These words, and turned away:

" *W. G. Williams, Engineers,*
  Killed in the final charge ! "

. . . .

Thus had I lain with Death, alone,
  Four hours in rain and mud,
Till, startled by the corporal's tone,
  I left that pool of blood !

Long years have flown since with the dead
   I spent that fearful night,
And I have marched, and fought, and bled
   In many a stirring fight;
I 've quailed before the leaden storm,
   But not with half such dread
As when unblanketing the form
   Of Captain Williams, dead !

LINES

SUGGESTED BY A CRAYON PORTRAIT OF MY YOUNGEST
DAUGHTER.

THY pensive eyes look down on me
    As here I sit alone,
And wonder if my thoughts of thee
    Find echo in thine own ;
Or if our spirits ever roam
    To mingle as of yore,
Thine from thy far-off Texas home,
    Mine from New England's shore.

I know thou often think'st of me,
    And of thy mother dear,
And haply o'er thy hours of glee
    Steals now and then a tear ;
For we do love thee, oh, so much !
    Yes, more than words can speak,
And pray that grief and care may touch
    Full lightly on thy cheek.

I know that thou hast borne a cross
    To sadden thy young heart ;
Thy parents, too, have known such loss, —
    They too were called to part
With one who for a period brief
    Had filled our home with joy,
And so can measure all thy grief
    For thy dead infant boy !

My thoughts go back, dear daughter mine,
    To thy bright infant days,
When I so loved that lisp of thine,
    And all thy winning ways.
Still further on, my darling girl,
    The moving picture goes,
And thou art with me in the whirl
    Of the Blue Mountain snows !

Next at the distant school, — glad hours
    Of visits dear to me,
When I could wander 'mong the flowers,
    And talk a while with thee, —
Who always grieved for home so blest,
    And mother's smile, dear heart !
Then laid thy head upon my breast
    And wept that we must part.

Once more, thy arms around my neck,
   I held that trembling form,
As from a frail bark's creaking deck
   We watched the ocean storm.
Fierce winds, mad waves, a fearful night, —
   No glimpse of moon or star, —
But, thank God! with the morning light
   We crossed the Brazos bar!

Last scene : beneath the marriage bell
   My precious daughter stood
With one whose noble heart could well
   Prize thee, the pure and good.
And now new cares, new hopes and fears
   Thy days and nights must fill ;
But still I know, through all the years,
   Thy heart is with us still.

What though thou 'rt distant from my sight,
   I know thou 'rt sometimes here,
And in the still hours of the night
   I wake and feel thee near;
And though thy semblance on the wall
   Seems all now left to me,
I know thy spirit heeds the call
   Whene'er I think of thee!
  8

www.ingramcontent.com/pod-product-compliance
Lightning Source LLC
Chambersburg PA
CBHW032112010726
47493CB00008B/2553